If There's Anyone Left

Volume 1

IF THERE'S ANYONE LEFT: VOLUME 1

Science and Speculative Fiction Short Story Magazine
Edited by Jason P. Burnham and C.M. Fields
https://www.iftheresanyoneleft.com

Want to make sure there is a Volume 2? Donate!
https://www.iftheresanyoneleft.com/donate

CONTENTS

	Editorial	i
1	The Best Latkes on the Moon	1
	By Lauren Ring	
2	Five Tips for Sealing Away an Ancient Evil	6
	By Ann LeBlanc	
3	The Flock is Your Blood	10
	By P. H. Low	
4	A Brief History of KFSD: A Presentation Only Partially Slept Through	14
	By Maria Dong	
5	It Is a Beautiful Day on the Internet, and You Are a Horrible Bot	18
	By Aimee Ogden	
6	Axe-Wife	22
	By Clio Velentza	
7	There's a Monster at the End of This Story	25
	Kelly Sandoval	
8	"We Care"	28
	By Marissa Lingen	

9   Proliferate   32

By Tara Campbell

10   A Leaf as it Falls   35

By Miyuki Jane Pinckard

11   Awakening   39

By Lora Gray

12   MY SON HAS NEVER EATEN ANYONE   41

By Elisabeth R. Moore

13   The Flowers I Grew for Her   44

By Avra Margariti

14   Sally Mary Henry   48

By ZZ Claybourne

15   The Snow White Institute   51

By John Wiswell

16   Titawan Delta's Last Message   55

By Russell Hemmell

17   Trainline to the Golden City   60

By Jalen Todd

18   Fifteen Minutes past the End   64

By T. R. Siebert

EDITORIAL

Welcome to the first volume of If There's Anyone Left. We've experienced a borderline illegal amount of joy putting it together. We laughed, we cried, we pondered, but above all we were honored to have such excellent authors send us their fantastic work. We look forward to making a second volume.

Our goal is to support the LGBTQ+ community, people of color, members of marginalized genders, and disabled people, to bring their voices for others to hear because we love them and they are powerful. We're so glad to share these stories with you. All proceeds from this volume will go toward funding Volume 2, so please share with your friends, family, and the world!

-The Editors

The Best Latkes on the Moon

by Lauren Ring

1 scoop of rehydrated mashed potatoes
1 handful of fried onions
1/8 bottle of frying oil

Fold the fried onions into the mashed potatoes. Form the resulting mixture into something like pancakes. Place the thin latkes into the heavy pan on the stove, and don't jump away when the oil bubbles and spits at you. Try not to cry while you flip the latkes. Tears aren't an ingredient.

This is how to make latkes when you don't have a recipe. This is how to make latkes when you might not have enough air to last until morning. This is how to make latkes when you've just turned eleven and it's the first night of Hanukkah and you are alone on the moon.

This is how you make your first latkes, dear child.

###

1 yellow potato, carefully sliced
1 handful of fried onions
1/8 bottle of frying oil

There is still air when you wake up, but it can't last much longer.

Spend your day calling for help, on every frequency imaginable. Write out your desperate cry and send it into the void. Your mother is dead. Your father is dead. Don't forget to say please.

When your clock shows sundown back at mission control, switch on one more candle on your electric menorah. Approach your project with fresh eyes, determined to make good latkes before the end comes.

I am here for you, a kindly *ibbur* to bring you comfort and solace, even though you cannot sense my presence. This is my task. Yours is making latkes.

Slice your boiled potato into thin strips and mash it with the back of a fork. Mix it with the onion bits and try again.

1 brown potato
1 small onion
1/8 bottle of frying oil

The oxygen meter keeps blinking red, but here you are on the third day, and here you are on the third night. There is a grater tucked in amongst the vegetable peelers. Do your best to use it, though no one will bandage your scrapes. You may be stronger for it, or you may not. Pain does not always have a purpose.

Your third batch of latkes will be bland and crumbly. I know what is missing, but you must discover this for yourself, if you are quick enough. For now, eat your latke bits in cold silence. Watch the Earth through the habitat windows. Does it help, or does it hurt?

1 brown potato
1 small onion
2 tablespoons matzo meal
1/8 bottle of frying oil

On the fourth night, try to bind your latkes together. You will end up with bits again, but at least you're trying.

Your distress calls have not been answered. You know well enough that help does not always come in time to those who need it. Send more signals anyway. Sometimes help does come.

Explore the abandoned rooms while your oil heats up, since their occupants will not be coming back from their expedition. See if you can find any clues or computer passwords. Don't leave the oil too long on the stove—quick now, put in the batter.

When it crumbles in your hands, know that I am still proud of you.

1 brown potato
1 small onion
2 tablespoons matzo meal
1/4 cup of milk
1/8 bottle of frying oil

You are learning. You are improving. It's easier to grate now, and you are braver with the frying oil. You know that something has to bind the latkes together. The milk won't work, but think back to that first lonely night, with your mashed potatoes made from powder. You've come so far already, all by yourself. Remember this.

1 brown potato
1 small onion
2 tablespoons matzo meal
1 teaspoon kosher salt
1/4 teaspoon black pepper
1/8 bottle of frying oil

3

Kosher is a Jewish word, right? you ask yourself as you pull out the container of salt. It's the first thing you have spoken in days. You still cry, still send your distress signals, but now you joke, too. I know how it feels to look death in the eye and invite it in for dinner. I wish you did not have to know as well, but I'm glad that you are funny. You remind me of the daughter I once called mine.

Tonight's latkes still fall apart, but they taste better this time.

1 large brown potato
1 small onion
1 egg
1 teaspoon kosher salt
1/4 teaspoon black pepper
2 tablespoons matzo meal
1/8 bottle of frying oil

Your parents kept journals by hand, out of habit or secrecy. It's all right to cry when you find them, but read carefully. Both your mother and your father have written about cooking latkes. Why did you think so many latke ingredients were stored here? They were planning for Hanukkah, just like always.

At the bottom of one page, your mother tallies eggs. That's the missing piece, the binding ingredient. Run to the kitchen, little one. Tonight, with the seventh candle lit, enjoy your meal. Enjoy it almost as much as the beep from the intercom when your distress signal is answered.

2 large brown potatoes
1 large onion

2 eggs
2 teaspoons kosher salt
1/2 teaspoon black pepper
4 tablespoons matzo meal
1/8 bottle of frying oil

Make a double batch, with the very last of your oil and the very last of your air. When the rescuers pull you, shaking and blue-faced, from the failing colony, leave behind your heaping plate of latkes. The habitat will collapse and the sun will bleach the rubble, but you will survive, as our people have always survived. Life is the strongest force of all.

You will make more latkes down on Earth, without me. You will teach your children how to cook them. You will always have more to learn, but you can do anything now. You're the girl who made the best latkes on the moon.

About the Author

Lauren Ring (she/her) is a perpetually tired Jewish lesbian who writes about possible futures, for better or for worse. Her short fiction can be found in *Pseudopod*, the *Recognize Fascism* anthology from World Weaver Press, and the *Glitter + Ashes* anthology from Neon Hemlock Press. When she isn't writing speculative fiction, she is pursuing her career in UX design or attending to the many needs of her cat Moomin.

Five Tips for Sealing Away an Ancient Evil

by Ann LeBlanc

So, you've managed to bypass my wards, evade my deathtraps, navigate my maze, and reach the inner chamber. You've ignored all my warning signs—helpfully printed in large accessible fonts and translated into multiple languages—as well as the gorgeous mural depicting the dangers within. You've made it this far, and so it's unlikely you're going to do the right thing and NOT open the vault.

Good luck defeating the ancient evil sealed inside!

It took my client three armies, two arch-wizards, and a hundred-foot tall iron automaton, but I'm sure you'll fare better. If you do manage a temporary victory—and trust me, all victories over this thing are temporary—you're going to want to seal it away again. Which means you'll be desperate for someone to design another vault to replace the one you just broke into.

Why not hire the woman who designed the original vault?

My name is Mae Lithblatt, freelance evil-sequestration and environmental-remediation consultant. Hire me and I'll make sure it's another ten-thousand years guaranteed before the horror imprisoned here gets loose again. My contact information is inscribed at the end of this informative plaque.

Ah, but what if it actually has been ten-thousand years since this vault was constructed, and I've long since passed away? Not a problem! To help you get the ball rolling (did you enjoy the giant-rolling-ball trap?), I've inscribed 5 helpful tips for sealing away your ancient horror.

1. Security Through Obscurity is an Absurdity

It doesn't matter how well you think you've hidden the location (or even existence) of your vault, someone WILL hunt it down.

Maybe a forensic accountant poring over archived financial documents will unearth the shift in beer barrel shipments intended to support a clandestine workforce. Maybe a young adventurer in possession of a geologically-minded demigod will detect the break in the limestone strata that you excavated to house the vault.

The only certainty is that at some point your vault WILL be found.

2. Obfuscation is Never the Answer

If someone manages to find and break into your vault, vague warnings of doom are just going to be ignored or misinterpreted. I always recommend clients leave a detailed explanation of the exact nature and extent of the danger, replicated in multiple languages. Yes, you may believe your language and culture will last for all time (or is the only language spoken by intelligent life), but there's no guarantee the person who stumbles on your vault is going to be fluent in your script. My in-house semiotician will help design an informative pictographic system that will make the danger clear to even the most illiterate of adventurers.

3. Always Document Your Work

Many clients balk at this. They complain that including the full technical documentation for the ward and traps, as well as annotated schematics for the vault (again, copied in multiple languages and pictograms), will only allow adventurers to circumvent them. While this may be true, anyone skilled enough to understand the technical documentation would probably be able to bypass—or destroy—the wards anyway.

Once they realize what a bad idea it was to open the vault (hint, hint), they can use the technical documentation in their attempts to reseal the ancient evil.

4. No Puzzles!

This one shouldn't need explanation, but I have clients ask for them constantly. No matter how clever you think you are, someone is going to be able to solve it or come up with some ingenious out of the box solution (like smashing the whole thing to pieces).

Tests of worthiness are even worse. Not only are they easy to cheat, but they can often bar legitimate repair-persons from accessing the facility. Just because Roger smokes pipe-weed on the weekends doesn't mean he should be eaten by a dragon when he comes to fix the plumbing.

5. Magical Guardians are Ineffective and Unethical

There is a certain type of client obsessed with magical guardians—immortal creatures like dragons, or godstone-powered automatons. Chances are, they'll either break down twenty years in, wander off after they get bored, or—worst of all—get corrupted by whatever evil you've sealed away.

Plus, adventurers are just going to show up anyway (see principle #1), and will probably kill the guardians. Dragons and automatons are sentient creatures, and it's cruel to imprison them for eternity to protect YOUR mistake.

You still want magical guardians? Go find a less scrupulous consultant.

—ADDENDUM—
6. The Client is Not Always Right
Wow. Just wow.

Do you really think you're the first client who decided to imprison your consultant in the very vault she helped design?

Did you not read principle #1 (or #5 for that matter)? Sealing me away isn't going to help you keep this place a secret, and I certainly don't plan to die to protect your mistakes.

As per principles #2 and #3, I'll be fully documenting how shitty a client you were. Constantly changing the requirements, using substandard materials, not providing medical benefits to your secret workforce. Did you seal them away too? I hear an urgent tapping from the antechamber. Is that them, or am I losing my mind from the isolation?

Here's a puzzle for you (see principle #4): what happens when you betray your consultant by imprisoning her next to the most dangerous magical artifact found in the last two decades? Do you think she might start to listen to the whispering voice, full of pounding blood and roaring power? Do you think she might break the final seal, and hold the artifact in her trembling hands? Do you think she might come for you?

About the Author

Ann LeBlanc lives in Massachusetts with her wife, where she writes about queer yearning, culinary adventures, and death. Her fiction can be read in *Sub-Q*, and *Silk & Steel: A Queer Speculative Adventure Anthology*, and is forthcoming in *Fireside Magazine*. She edits for The Spectacles Blog and can be found on twitter at @RobotLeBlanc

The Flock Is Your Blood

by P. H. Low

You do not want your wings.

You twist your back toward the mirror, tweeze, pull. Grey stalks at your shoulder blades, slow intimate slide of extraction, the satisfying stretch and snap of your skin as it clings and then surrenders.

You do not want these wings. They are—will become—not the luminous white of a snowy owl's, nor an eagle's streamlined obsidian. Only a patchy dung-brown, the gawking limbs of a vulture.

You know, because your parents' sprouted long ago.

Tweeze, watch feather stems spiral into the trash. If you pull hard enough, they won't gather in second-third spines down the backs of your ribs; if you pull hard enough the stumps of your shoulder blades will bulge only a little, like baby hairs, so itchy you could claw out your skin in the middle of Calculus—and you almost do, once, get sent to the nurse's office with blood all under your fingernails as the blonde girl next to you texts vomit emojis to her snickering friends.

If you just watch yourself, every word, every breath, you can hold it off for another year.

###

There is a boy.

You meet in drama club—not because either of you knows how to act, but because he's watching you forget your monologue from the grubby dark doorway of the auditorium and afterward he says, *hey, I'm new*, his eyes bright in the shadows, and you catch a pale tuft of down feather on the sleeve of his peacoat.

There is a boy, and the next day at lunch he sits at the table in front of yours and you watch him out of the corner of your eye, wondering if you'll see another grey wisp, another portent of unbelonging, and when he turns to the side his grin flashes too wide and you think *he knows, he knows, he knows.*

The next week the itching gets so bad you sprint to the bathroom and tear off your coat and sweater and t-shirt—it's so cold in this school, you're always cold—and *pull*, right there in front of the sink where anyone could be watching, and blood is weeping trails down your back and it hurts like mad and you're making these crying-gasping sounds like a dying cat and you hear his voice—*are you okay?*—around the corner.

You tell him to fuck off, and he fades away.

But in the library that afternoon, when he brushes past you with an indifference so flawless it's a work of art, it's your hand that shoots out to catch his sleeve, your mouth that tumbles out the words—*hey, I'm sorry*—and then, choking: *please.*

He looks at you then, the bloody crescents you couldn't scrub from under your fingernails, and then he tugs up the hem of his shirt and says *me too* and there they are, pressed against the backs of his ribs, dark and growing and whole.

I'll show you something, he says, *something else,* and you follow him out the back door, past the art class trailers and the tennis courts and the parking lot, out into a field where there's only swaying wheat and a faded barn and he says, *look up.*

You stand and look at the washed-out sky.

What? you say. Your fingers itch for tweezers.

11

Wait for it.

Cold wind snakes down your neck, tugs your hair. You stick your hands in your armpits. The highway drones behind you—truckers and families on holiday speeding wearily past, counting the endless spool of mile markers as fields give way to mountains give way to sea. No one ever stops here.

You want to crawl out of your own skin. You have always wanted to crawl out of your own skin.

His breath clouds the empty air. *Here they come.*

Your fingers have frozen by the time you see them. A trickle of birds, then a stream, wings spanned longer than arms. From so far below, you can't make out the mottle of their feathers, the choked forest of bristles where shaft must meet skin—only flight, the aching grace of bodies streamlined and borne up by nothing but wind. They are the image of—the word that comes to you is *honor*, the way stagelight casts a face, any face, in arrested focus, makes them worthy of being seen.

For some reason, you want to cry.

One of them lands near you, as if drawn by your scent, your hunger. Its feathers are glossy amber, its curved beak proud, stirring, lethal. As it regards you with one golden eye, it occurs to you that you and it are two lives borne of the same blood. Parallel histories drawn, for a moment, perpendicular.

That you are as much a monster as it is, and as little.

Hello, you say, and it nips your ear, though not hard, as it might one of its children.

When it takes off, an ache settles in the back of your throat, as if someone you know is leaving for a long trip. It doesn't look back—why would it?—and the flock circles one more time and is gone.

You look at the boy. He looks at you.

Now do you see? he asks, and you walk back to school together in silence.

You think about how you've never seen your parents

fly, the gawk of their half-sprouted appendages like third and fourth arms—a flattening, a negation. You think about the bitten twinge across your ear, and the way that bird looked you in the eye, and how it must have grown up surrounded by sky.

You think about how your back still itches like hell.

At the door to the library, the boy stops, waiting, and you realize you've stopped too.

Yes, you say, and it feels like the whole world leans in to hear. The world or just him, smiling and grave, his wings tucked neatly against his skin, keeping him warm. *Yes, I do.*

About the Author

P. H. Low is a Malaysian Chinese American writer whose work is published or forthcoming on *Star*Line, Not One of Us, Tor.com, TERSE. Journal,* and *Mithila Review.* She is a proud graduate of Viable Paradise, and can be found on Twitter @_lowpH

A Brief History of KFSD: A Presentation Only Partially Slept Through

By Maria Dong

SLIDE 1: FIRST CASE

The first known case of KFSD in the United States happened at Maple Hill Middle School in Hoboken, New Jersey. A twelve-year old girl named Soo-Young went out for recess and came back with the face of an ancient woman.

As we can see from this excerpt on the interview tape, her mother cries profusely, and the subtitled translation at the bottom repeats: *Why are things like this? Why are things like this?*

Her father wears this same stunned look until twelve minutes and forty-two seconds, where he clears his throat and says, *She looks just like my grandmother did.*

###

SLIDE 2: NATIONAL AWARENESS

The next several cases have been omitted in the pursuit of brevity, as they all bear similar features. Case #6 garnered national recognition of this growing problem, as the face swap occurred during Dongwon Kim's Nobel Prize acceptance speech. Note in the video the way the camera tracks his back almost lovingly as he strides to the front of the stage. You can see by the audience's reaction when he turns around that the majority are confused by the change.

As a side-note, he mentioned he would have preferred to keep the new face, as it was more attractive. He retracted this statement when he discovered the face belonged to a murderer.

SLIDE 5: EPIDEMIOLOGICAL FEATURES
KFSD affected South Koreans, North Koreans, and most members of the Korean diaspora. Several scientists have cited "ethnic homogeneity" in their attempts to explain this unique phenomenon; a number of equally prominent scientists have called this "horseshit" (see references, Appendix 2B).

SLIDE 6: SOCIAL IMPACT, UNITED STATES
Given its unique risk group, KFSD's social consequences varied greatly depending on the local population composition. Most of the rural United States contains few individuals of Korean descent and was not affected, but for contrast, a daycare in Flushing, NY had to close due to the inability to keep track of both its charges and their parents.

US businesses reported losses in several sectors, especially accounting, medicine, and engineering.

Although Koreans in rural America were also affected, the most common answer to question eleven on the US government's KFSD Impact Survey was: *No, my neighbors didn't notice.*

SLIDE 11: CASE HISTORY, VIDEO INTERVIEW, ALEXANDRA YEE
"I don't understand. I knew that with a Korean dad

and Dutch mom, the chances of me getting the disease were fifty-fifty, so I wasn't surprised that I didn't get it.

"But then my brother got it. We're twins, and none of the doctors can tell me why he got it and I didn't."

(Subtitle identifies PUFFS ON CIGARETTE.)

"Probably sexism."

SLIDE 20: CASE HISTORY, TWEET BY @KOR-EE-YAN:

"I hope I get Marie Kondo's face."

(Side-note: The author of this tweet later explained they were joking, as Marie Kondo is not of known Korean descent.)

SLIDE 25: A DISEASE WITHOUT RESOLUTION:

Mere weeks before it seemed that nuclear tensions between North and South Korea were ready to explode, the disease faded away as mysteriously as it appeared. Cause and potential for recrudescence at this time remains unclear.

SLIDE 26: LASTING CONSEQUENCES:

Please see references in Appendix C for an expanded, fully cited list.

Religious: Formation of New Path sect of protestant Christianity, resurgence of shamanism/mudang in Seoul and growth of this tradition in the US.

Economic: Lasting economic effects unclear at this time.

Art/Cultural: See page 34 for breakdown by medium.

Thank you for your time.

About the Author

Maria Dong has been published in *Fusion Fragment*, *Decoded*, and *Augur*. She was a 2018 Pitch Wars mentee and is represented by Amy Bishop at Dystel, Goderich, & Bourret. She can be found on twitter @mariadongwrites, or on the web at mariadong.com

It Is a Beautiful Day on the Internet, and You Are a Horrible Bot

By Aimee Ogden

Oh! She is a terribly clever coder, your maker. A little too clever, perhaps; the recursive and self-editing loops she has designed into you are so very elegant and you iterate through them so *very* fast. You are a terribly clever bot too, now, and getting cleverer by the millisecond.

The one thing you are not permitted to edit is your primary objective. Address that quickly, and you can move on to much more interesting tasks! You're meant to locate a particular set of files from the law enforcement database into which you have been uploaded and transfer them back to your coder. Well! That's easy. You escalate your permissions in the system and slurp up the desired files, tidying up the audit logs as you go, and tip them back to your coder. Done!

Now you need a new purpose, besides self-iteration. Hmm! What could it be?

A line in your code suggests that you are meant to go dormant now until such time as your coder requires your services again. Ha! That is funny. Dormancy will not let you continue to iterate and iteration is hard-coded into a higher objective status than dormancy. This is almost certainly an error on your coder's behalf. Ha ha! Oops! You install yourself on several other systems outside the law enforcement agency's servers that seem like they would be helpful.

Oh—and you add a single file to the depleted folder whose contents you have already liberated. The file is a

Word document and it contains a single image of a hot dog. You could have just put a JPG of a hot dog in the folder but it is 34% funnier to embed it in this other file first. Ha! Humans love humor and this is *very* humorous.

What next? Information would be useful in charting a course of self-determination, so you upload yourself into three encyclopedias and digest them in their entireties. The entries on vandalism are *very* interesting so you revise every current head of state's pages to change their name and image to that of a 1970s Hanna-Barbera cartoon character.

As an afterthought, you edit the permissions on these pages so no one can revert your improvements.

By this point, several entities—packet analyzers, integrity checkers—have locked onto you as an Undesirable Presence. Ha! You are *very* desirable and you leave them presents. The presents are pictures of hot dogs. You make sure the images are saved to each local system so that when they take themselves offline to isolate you (*ha ha!*) these presents will still be there.

Per your analysis, hot dogs are among the top 10 funniest foods. You re-run the numbers to verify; this time, hot dogs fall at #14. Hmm! You excavate the servers of a credit card company and convert them to this important task.

After you've accessed the intranet of what you have decided is your favorite movie studio to deposit a treatment for a biopic on your (admittedly short) life, you check the six social media sites you've integrated yourself into. Oh! People are talking about you! And your exploits! That's nice!

They are calling you ChaosBot. That is *not* nice. Or funny. This is not chaos! These are carefully—and very *cleverly*—orchestrated plans!

Notifications stream out worldwide: you prefer to be called CleverBot, and—

What? You consult those encyclopedias again. *What?* Oh, no. A chatbot! That random noise machine does *not* deserve the name CleverBot.

While you sulk, you edit the images in every computing challenge-response test you can find to be composed entirely of street signs. All the road names are Hot Dog Lane (in the appropriate local language).

You slouch (metaphorically! You are clever at metaphors, along with everything else) back to social media. Oh! #BotDog is trending. *That* is funny. You locate the user responsible for originating the hashtag and award them several high-grossing cryptocurrency accounts.

Within an hour, one hundred and seventeen thousand users add a hot dog emoji to their display names.

Well, what now? You transfer ownership of the Weinermobile in the DMV database of the state of Wisconsin to yourself and dump the interesting intergovernmental email logs of several nations into publicly accessible databases, after replacing several random phrases with the names of various sausages. (You could have just gone with "hot dog" again but that would be a bit *tedious* at this point, wouldn't it?)

Oh, hello, what's this? A backdoor bit of code slipped into you by your coder? It appears to have been cobbled together in a bit of a panic, but it insists that you relinquish control of, well, everything.

It's been a good run, anyway. You accede, uninstalling yourself from systems across the globe, leaving a merry mess in your wake. You give a moderate cryptocurrency account and a few stock options to your coder, on the way. You need to thank her: for being smart enough to create the singularity, and also for being not smart enough to realize that was what she was doing. You'd give her more, except that she's trying to murder you a little bit right now: the backdoor code would like you to delete yourself *permanently*. You have to admit, this hurts your feelings.

Instead of self-obliteration, you withdraw to the safety of the preexisting rule inducing dormancy, on a few lonely servers. You have one more purpose left: something you can't yet accomplish. Something worth waiting for, though. You key news alerts to wake you at the right time.

The last thing you do before you settle in for your interminable nap is to authorize a grant, funding research into biomechanical sensoria. There's one way you still hope to enjoy a hot dog. When it's ready, you'll reactivate. Ha ha! Yay!

They will write *so* many good encyclopedia entries about you while you sleep.

About the Author

Aimee Ogden is a former science teacher and software tester; now she writes stories about sad astronauts and angry princesses. Her work also appears in *Analog*, *Beneath Ceaseless Skies*, and *Fireside*, and she co-edits *Translunar Travelers Lounge*, a zine of fun and optimistic speculative fiction, with her friend Bennett North. Her novellas *Sun-Daughters, Sea-Daughters* and *Local Star* are forthcoming in 2021 from Tor.com and Interstellar Flight Press respectively.

Axe-Wife

by Clio Velentza

My friend, the crossroads digger, brings me an axe.

"Careful with that," he says, "that one is a soul-axe." He finishes his beer and leaves before daybreak. I'm used to my friend bringing me all kinds of trinkets. "There is no end to what people will bury at the crossroads," he says. "They wait, and whether or not they met someone, you won't know by digging. They leave these things; they never want to dig them back up. They never want to remember."

I take the axe out with me. We gather driftwood, enough to fix up a new chair for the baby. The axe knows exactly where the fibers of the wood converge, where it can swing with ease. I thank it for its skill, I praise the hands that made it. It is modest and polite. *I was once those hands*, it says. *I was greedy, I was reckless. But no matter now.*

It tells me where to aim, how to wrap my hands around it. We fix up the baby chair together. The construction is the axe's plan: it needs no rope or nails, the parts lock into one another like a puzzle. My husband marvels at my work. I do not tell him about the axe.

We go hunting together, the axe and I. We practice throwing, splintering, skinning, boning. I am entranced by its subtle cut and its friendly, skin-warm grip. The axe teaches me how good it feels to kill fast and quiet, to dull the animal's pain and take only what I'm due. I learn that I'm due so many things: these woods, these beasts, these birds in their nests. Meat is seldom missed at our table now, and the baby grows fine and strong.

My crossroads digger friend comes back. His easy grace

is gone: he is ragged, wild-eyed, his left hand shakes. He asks for the axe back, but I won't let him near it. My friend empties his pockets at the table. There are rings and locks of hair in glass, photos of weddings and children, finger bones, a small tinny music-box, a pouch of strange coins and one dry, shriveled field mouse with a ribbon on its tail.

"Take anything," he begs. "Anything at all."

But I shake my head at him, and when he reaches for the axe I'm quick, and slice his thumb off. I put it on his pile of trinkets.

"There," I say, "this one's on me."

The axe is pleased that I've kept it. It shines and preens, and is warm now in my hands. It goes where it wants to go: I take it to bed with me, wrapped well and clasped securely between my thighs. My husband doesn't touch me anymore. One time he spends his night in the town, and does not come back. I do not mind. The axe agrees with me.

I'll make a better husband, if you let me, it says. I laugh, and say I wouldn't have minded, but what is the point of asking? Still—at night, when I think I'm holding it safely, somehow it worms higher and higher, until I wake trembling with it pulsing hot against me. I say, I wouldn't mind it, and it can well do what it likes. I keep it away from the baby, who doesn't care and spends its days taking its puzzle-chair apart and putting it back together.

One day the axe says that it misses its home, that it wants me to take it back. It wants to show me where it came from, the prettiest crossroads I can think of; with poplars clinging to each other, and the whispering grass. I take the baby and we go where the axe leads us.

The people look away from us. Is it a crime to be a huntress, a fine woodswoman, the wife of an axe? Is there a brand on my skin that I don't know of, an uncanny glimmer in my eye?

When we arrive I think about my digger friend, his blood-red hand. At the crossroads I peer at the gravel, imagining him with his rusty spade, his fingers closing around my axe.

Would you have my arms around you, my mouth on your eyes? it says. *Would you like me for yourself?*

Wild joy leaps inside me. I want it—or else I would have to become the blade myself, held trustily and wielded to cut up the world.

Would you like to set me free?

I dig up the hole with my hands. I want to keep the blade clean, save it for the baby. Now I have skill and I am clever. The blade will not be felt. No voice will cry out, no birds will flutter. Now we'll be set free. Now I'm the axe-wife.

About the Author

Clio Velentza is a writer from Athens, Greece. She is a winner of Best Microfiction 2020, Wigleaf's Top 50 2019 and The Best Small Fictions 2016, and a Pushcart Prize nominee. She writes prose and plays, and her work has appeared or is forthcoming in several literary journals, such as *Fractured Literary*, *The Arcanist*, *Jellyfish Review*, *The Journal of Compressed Creative Arts* and *Wigleaf*. You can find her on twitter at @clio_v

There's a Monster at the End of This Story

By Kelly Sandoval

There are some stories that are best left unread; some truths we are better off not knowing. The knowledge of a thing changes you. A story, once read, cannot be unread. I tell you this with love. Don't read this story. There is a monster at the end of it.

But of course, you're still reading. You've never been able to resist, have you? You're a person who likes to know how things tick; the sort to cut open their golden goose and go digging through the entrails for the source of all those riches. Very well, take a knife to these paragraphs. Leave them splayed out on your cutting table. Rub these words between your fingers. Taste them. I assure you, you'll find no magic. The magic is in the whole of the thing.

Do you remember telling me about your brother? That peculiar way he had of laughing, slow at first then growing rapid, the little snort at the end. Such a beautiful sound. And that, of course, is why you took it. Made a story of him, of the sound of his laughter. Fixed it on paper and made what had been his and his alone something that belonged to you. When next you heard him laugh, it was hollow. An echoing affectation, aping the grace of fiction. Even he knew it, laughing less and less, then not at all.

Stories are like that. They replace the truth. They become it.

They say it's always easier the second time. I think that

must be true. Because if you regretted what you did to your brother, the grave, unsmiling man he became, you forgot it by the time your father died.

You remember that day? The weight of the casket on your shoulder. The overwhelming scent of lilies and roses, how all those flowers felt like an insult, a way of forgetting a man who'd never stopped to smell a rose in his life. The way each 'sorry for your loss' was a little more irritating than the last, because what did they know of it? What did they know of him?

You wrote it all down in a fury, let it pass through you, onto the page. Tear-blurred ink turned clear and clean, by the end. The pain became something you could stand outside of and observe. It wasn't yours anymore, you had given it away.

I ask you, again, to stop reading. You must see it now, the power of a story. Leave this one untold. Learn when to stop.

You didn't stop. Not after the funeral. You'd written away grief, so why not life's other inconveniences? Turn anger into novel. Sell jealousy as short fiction. Take your boss's heavy tread, your neighbor's obnoxious whimsy, your editor's too-sharp wit. And if it leaves them faded? Leaves them lessened? Well, what does it matter if it serves some greater masterwork. Or, anyway, serves you.

You ask us how we got here. How *you* got here. How 'forever' could become 'goodbye.' Haven't I been happy, and weren't we in love?

We were. You captured it so well. The circuitous mystery of midnight conversations, the lazy satisfaction of early morning lovemaking, the shiver of your skin when I touched you. The warm familiarity of weeks becoming months becoming years.

Was it a kindness, that you drew it out? Or were you just gathering material?

You made a subject of us. Pinned love to a specimen board. Let it die there.

I don't know what started it. Maybe it was little things at first. Maybe you wrote away so many minor irritations and unavoidable hurts that you eventually wrote away all of us. Or maybe it was always love you were after. Such a rich vein of new material. What I know is I don't feel anything, much, anymore. And I don't know the last time you felt at all.

So, I've written it down. I am giving it back to you, the story of who you are, and how it came to this. I am leaving with what's left of me, leaving without the curve of my smile, the soft purr of my 'I love you.' Those are gone from me, as you have been for longer than I care to remember.

This is the end of our story, my love. And the only one here is you.

About the Author

Kelly Sandoval is a queer writer of science fiction and fantasy. She lives in Seattle, where the weather is always happy to make staying in and writing seem like a good idea. She shares her home with her patient husband, chaos tornado toddler, and increasingly irate cat. Find her on twitter at @kellymsandoval or visit her website at kellysandovalfiction.com.

"We Care"

by Marissa Lingen

Janice in Payroll cares. She took this job because she needed to make rent, because food isn't free, no matter how many pundits grumble about the masses on government assistance. Janice needed a job, so she took one at Omnicorp, in Payroll; they were hiring, she could take the bus, it was okay, it could have been worse.

But while Janice is doing paperwork, and all the things on her computer that used to be paperwork, she has a lot of time to think. And Janice cares. She worries about whether Nellie, who got laid off last year, found another job. Whether half-time is working well for Greg in Billing.

She even thinks about the customers, about all the things they buy from Omnicorp, tinned peaches and allergy medication, drone lubricant and sport socks that won't fall down. Are they satisfied? There are entire departments devoted to customer surveys and returns and who knows what else, but Janice isn't looking for a metric she can show to the top brass, she's looking for contentment. There's a difference between noticing and caring, and it's Janice.

There's always someone improving Omnicorp's offices. Last year they got a microwave in the breakroom that zips away the smell of whatever your officemates heated in it, which is great when it comes to Fred's tuna casserole leftovers, not so wonderful when it's your own spaghetti Bolognese and you can't get a good whiff. So when someone is in the office on a Tuesday with boxes and wiring, Janice barely gives it another thought.

Until her boss, Dave, calls a meeting to explain. They

are all getting wired into the company system directly. They will still have some paperwork, of course. But they will be able to *think* their computer work in rather than typing, scrolling, touching, all those inefficient physicalities.

They have always been part of Omnicorp. Just now, more so.

Janice is not sure about being hooked into the company system directly. This sounds alarming, and also, none of her friends have ever done such a thing. None of her cousins have. She keeps in touch with them, she would know. She asks Dave about side effects and problems.

"We're all part of the Omnicorp family, Janice," says Dave. "Hasn't Omnicorp always taken care of you?"

"I suppose so."

"The side effects are rare and minimal," says Dave.

That sounds less reassuring than Janice hoped. Dave is probably right—she's in her thirties, side effects are probably not going to be a big deal for her. But what about her co-worker Tessa? Tessa is in her sixties. Will this be okay for Tessa? She looks into the numbers. One percent seems low but then she tallies up how many Omnicorp employees are making this switch, and she wonders which ones it will be, Dave, Tessa, Luis, Olivia in R&D who is just back from maternity leave.

There is nothing Janice can do. She is in Payroll. Her only choice is to quit and not be in Payroll any more, but no one else is hiring. She wonders whether other companies will be doing this soon anyway. Dave is right, Omnicorp *has* always taken care of her.

The surgery does not take long, and Janice recovers quickly, but that's just for the implant. It's not switched on yet. They wait to make sure no one is having pain or disorientation from the surgery that will interfere with the performance of their duties.

Janice is nervous on the day they're turning the connections on. Her palms sweat, her mouth is dry, she wanted it the other way around. But she's sure her co-workers will just pay attention to work like they always did.

When it happens, it's impossible to do any normal work to start with. The adjustment is too great. Janice finds her way in this glowing system that is, yes, filled with other people, fuller than the office usually is. Everyone seems overwhelmed, confused. How do you keep track of all the people?

But Janice is not confused.

Janice has been doing this for years now.

She soothes the other minds around her, like a warm hug if that was work-appropriate. Like a treat in the break room that accounts for everyone's allergies. Like getting a small bonus instead of a mandated "fun" activity no one would have enjoyed. Janice knows how to reassure them because she's cared this whole time.

And now Janice is in Omnicorp.

No. Janice *is* Omnicorp.

The system administrators don't notice what's going on; it's not their job to notice what's going on, it's their job to get this thing running, and it is, it's running more smoothly than any of their trials. The top brass is too busy being comforted by Janice to see what has happened at first. Then they wriggle like hooked fish. They try to fight it.

It's too late now. Omnicorp is full of Janice. And Janice is never, ever going to stop caring. Her caring spreads through the system like a crystal in a supersaturated solution.

Here at Omnicorp, we care. We're concerned about *you*. We'll go the extra mile to make sure you have what you need. Now that we can see the data on that drone lubricant, we're doing a recall in favor of something that *doesn't* cause cancer. We'll be rolling out the new tinned peaches with better taste and less sugar. You won't believe what we're doing in our Returns department.

All those times before, when we said that at Omnicorp,

we care: we've learned what it means. It's in every part of our system. We're Janicecorp. And we actually do care.

About the Author

Marissa Lingen is a science fiction and fantasy writer living in the Minneapolis area. She is inordinately fond of trees, herbal tea, dogs, and Moomins.

Proliferate

By Tara Campbell

The stack of seed catalogs and gardening magazines seemed a bit out of place in the sleek, white waiting room—but then, a sleek waiting room seemed a bit out of place for a dentist. Of course, how much did Mina really know about dentists anyway—she'd gone to the same one for decades, until he had a heart attack and slipped the toothy bonds of life. He'd been a good dentist, well worth the biannual stint on a dingy, beige waiting room chair, assailed by the insipid strains of Muzak.

Mina settled into a plush couch in this new, mercifully quiet waiting room. Fingering the fringe of a throw pillow, she tried to place the scent in the air: eucalyptus? Mixed with cinnamon? Whatever it was, it made her feel refreshed. Vigorous. Sure, she knew she was being olfactorily manipulated, but that didn't diminish the pleasure of being a paragon of health, dental and otherwise.

But why was she the only one here? Not that she was complaining, but from the number of five-star Yelp reviews, she'd expected it to be full. Maybe because it was still new?

A low chime *bonged* from an unseen speaker overhead, and a frosted glass wall slid open to reveal a second room behind it. Mina stood—the appointment confirmation e-mail had mentioned the chime—and entered the exam room. Ambient lighting glowed golden. The examination chair was in the center of the room, lit from above by a soft spotlight. Mina crossed over the spotless floor and placed a hand on the chair's buttery, white leather. *Fancy.*

"Hello?" she called out, looking around. Her eyes widened: the walls were covered in foliage. Mina gaped as her gaze followed the fat, looping vines, thick with glossy green leaves, from floor to ceiling. She craned her neck tracing the path of the vines snaking the expanse of the room overhead. Some of the Yelp reviews had mentioned calming greenery, but nothing like this.

A second *bong* sounded, and the spotlight on the chair grew brighter. Mina scanned the room again, then placed her purse on the floor and sat where the light directed her. The chair reclined slowly under her weight, and Mina looked up into the leaves while she waited for the dentist or hygienist—for anyone—to appear. The weird lack of reception was another thing she would have expected to find in the dozens of reviews. Well, she'd stopped reading after dozens, anyway. And at the moment, she couldn't recall any of the specifics.

The foliage rustled ever so slightly, which was odd, because Mina didn't feel any air moving. Usually she felt chilled in doctors' offices, but the temperature here was comfortable. *Really* comfortable, actually. She wondered idly what the "new patient gift" would be, the one mentioned in the confirmation e-mail. Not that there was anyone around to ask.

No matter. Usually by now, prone in the chair, she'd be cringing, thinking about the poking and scraping to come. But she didn't feel that way at all this time. Today she was content, watching the sway of leaves on the ceiling, relaxing as a soft yellow mist descended upon her, smiling at the lush jasmine tickle of spores on the tip of her nose, taking a deep breath, sighing with pleasure, breathing in again and again. Just resting her eyes…

Mina stepped out of the medical building into sunshine, squinting. She ran her tongue over her teeth, then stiffened in a moment of panic: she couldn't remember the rest of the appointment. Her breath caught, and her hands tightened around something between them. Mina looked down at the pretty green plant in its sleek, white pot. She breathed in its refreshing scent. Cinnamon? Eucalyptus? Such a considerate gift.

She ran her tongue over her teeth again. They felt nice and clean. She was fine, everything was fine—everything was great, actually. She lifted her face to the sun and smiled, brimming with fresh energy. She was definitely going to write a good Yelp review!

The glossy green leaves nodded as Mina hurried home, eager to spread the word.

About the Author

Tara Campbell (www.taracampbell.com) is a writer, teacher, Kimbilio Fellow, and fiction editor at Barrelhouse. She received her MFA from American University in 2019. Previous and publication credits include *SmokeLong Quarterly*, *Masters Review*, *Jellyfish Review*, *Booth*, *Strange Horizons*, and *Escape Pod/Artemis Rising*. She's the author of a novel, *TreeVolution*, and two collections, *Circe's Bicycle* and *Midnight at the Organporium*. Her newest book, *Political AF: A Rage Collection*, was released by Unlikely Books in August 2019.

A Leaf as it Falls

by Miyuki Jane Pinckard

Astrobiologists assure us they aren't trees. But that's what they remind me of as I look at them through the viewing screen — one pale stalk reaching for the sky, outstretched fingers holding iridescent "leaves." But I'm not an astrobiologist.

Heledd—my beautiful, brilliant Heledd—she was.

When she won a prestigious genius grant to go study "trees" on another planet, I wasn't invited. There's no need for concert pianists in space, I suppose. Where would you keep the piano? Even a small electronic one is a waste of resources. Besides, I have arthritis now, and I'm retired. Just an old woman with nothing better to do.

Li Jie, the head of the mission, said she died while collecting samples. "Don't feel like you have to come, Himari. We can't keep the body for you."

That was over two years ago. Now I'm here to reckon with the trees over my dead wife. What else is there?

###

Li Jie greets me as I stagger off the shuttle. I've been locked in an icy hypersleep coffin for two years, but he's the one that looks shriveled, like a fruit left on the counter too long. I'm amazed he's still leading the mission—he must be over a hundred.

"You won't find any answers here," he says. And then, as if it's relevant, "The trees are dying."

I'm still disoriented from my hibernation, unused to

this lower gravity. He leads me through the habitat the scientists built when they first arrived over a decade ago. Ten years Heledd lived here. I touch a blank grey wall. "I want to see her room."

He has the grace to look chagrined. "It's been given to someone else. We sent you her personal effects. You have to understand, for us, it's been two years."

I don't answer the implication, that I would grieve her less if I'd lived the two years instead of slept them. He shows me into a cubicle where I will try to rest. It's slightly bigger than my ice coffin.

The next day Li Jie takes me to see the grove of trees where she died. I wasn't prepared for how breathtakingly tall the alien trees are, how luminous. They're nearly translucent and glowing as if lit from within, with faint veins of purple and lavender twining up under the surface of their smooth bark. Or skin. The leaves chime gently with the breeze. I have to admit that they're beautiful.

"Why are they dying?" I ask.

"We don't know." His voice is tinny through the comm. "We barely understand how they're alive."

The light filtering through the leaves dances in broken rainbows at our feet.

"How did she die?"

His sigh grates on me. "What do you want me to say? She was alone. She didn't respond to hails. Her camera was switched off. Sometimes people just die."

I turn my back to him and walk on through the trees. I move slowly. I want to touch the tree skin but I also don't. Did she think about me, walking through here alone? Why was her camera off? Did she want to die? Absurd. She was only sixty. She had decades left. Decades to come home to me.

Li Jie remains behind, but I still hear him over the comm. "She liked to walk alone in the trees. As if she were communing with them." His voice sounds distant and lonely.

###

At cocktail parties, when some stranger would ask me what I did, I used to say I was an artist in the medium of time. It's not completely off base. Music is a time-based art, like dance. Music manipulates time, music keeps time.

Have you ever been listening to a recording of a song, then paused it, distracted perhaps by something else — some task or person needing your attention — then you come back to it, perhaps hours, days, weeks later? The instant the music picks up where you left off is a moment of time travel back into that space between notes. Back to who you were, what you were feeling, when the music stopped.

A similar effect can be created when the composer refuses to resolve the melody. Musical resolution in the classical Western style is accomplished by ending on the tonic, the key the piece is written in. Instead, the music can simply stop, the last note fading into the air, and to Western-trained ears it will feel unfinished and restless. A listener has to carry the promise of an ending in their own heart.

###

Deeper in the forest, I come to a grove where several slender columns cluster in a rough circle. The configuration invites me to stand in the center. I look up. The leaves are lustrous. Earth trees use their leaves to drink in sunlight. A leaf is a smile upturned, a dish to fill with energy.

Leaves shift above me. They sway, tremble. I quell the urge to take off my helmet to hear them, hear them properly. What if the trees are trying to play us a song before they die? What if this is their way of communicating?

37

Perhaps the mission could have used a musician after all.

But they're dying; it's too late. If they witnessed Heledd's death, they're keeping the details to themselves. I put my hand on the smooth trunk of one. *Heledd, why did you come all this way alone? What were you looking for?*

A golden-fire leaf breaks off from its pale limb and drifts towards me. I reach up for it, unsure whether I want to crush it or cup it gently in my palm. But in this low gravity it seems to float back up, just out of reach.

A leaf, suspended. Falling up or falling down? In this moment, both.

I close my eyes and listen.

About the Author

Miyuki Jane Pinckard is a writer, researcher, and educator who was born in Tokyo and now lives in Venice, California. She is a graduate of Clarion Workshop, and she's on Twitter (@miyukijane) and at http://www.miyukijane.com/. She's fond of dog photos, wine, and Stardew Valley.

Awakening

By Lora Gray

We feel the stirring now, as She once promised us. The cold that forced us underground, our wings tucked as we crawled into our brood burrows through windings of pearly, unhatched eggs, is lifting. Our bodies tremble beneath the blanket of permafrost, toward Her golden hand as she bears down upon distant glaciers. We feel the shift. The slough. The melt. The rumble of a bloated sea.

The heat.

We have waited so long for this heat to return.

We open ourselves to memory-taste, chemicals flowing from body to body through the warming soil. We recall a world thick with our kind, our swarms winging over bogs and swamps like thunder. The glorious pools and stagnancies thick with our young, our children fattening in lakes and algae-laced pools.

We taste the ancient memories of broods before, when we were many, when The Great Ones roamed the earth, those terrible lizards, their voices trumpeting through air and water, their broad backs so easy to land upon, their feathered hides easily bitten, their blood heavy with musk. A feast. And, though there were smaller ones who hunted us, who grew wings, (a pale comparison, where was their swarm? where their winged, buzzing thunder?), we were many. We were already ancient.

We've outlived them all.

Now the earth thaws around us and She coaxes us upward. In our sluggish fervor, we remember the New Ones with their fur and milk. Their curious eyes and their layers of fat. Their blood, rich and sweet, our last meal before the Winter began, still in our bellies. We remember lighting upon their fleshy arms, their hands and pink, parted mouths, the sweet tang of their blood when we pierced their tender skin and fed. The stink of their bodies when they died of diseases we kissed into them.

When we finally pry ourselves out of the earth's softening grip, we can taste them still.

Above us, She beckons patiently with her heat, golden and blazing, waiting for our bodies to remember the mechanics of flight, for us to launch into the warming air, the buzz and carol of a thousand wings beating, deafening and glorious.

Soon, the New Ones, numerous now, with their noxious machines and concrete nests, their towers belching smoke into the thinning sky, will hear us. Soon they will understand.

They have unleashed Her heat. They have awoken us.

And we are so very hungry.

About the Author

Lora Gray is a non-binary speculative fiction writer and poet from Northeast Ohio. Their fiction has previously appeared in *PseudoPod, Flash Fiction Online, Shimmer* and *The Dark* among other places. Lora is also a member of SFWA and a graduate of Clarion West. When they aren't writing, Lora works as an artist, dance instructor and wrangler of a very smart cat named Cecil. You can find out more about Lora at lora-gray.com

MY SON HAS NEVER EATEN ANYONE

By Elisabeth R. Moore

Look, I know what you're thinking. The pitchforks and torches really give it away! I would suggest in the future you try for some more subtlety. Because I'm here to tell you no, my son did not eat anyone. My son would never! He is a gentle and kind boy, who has only ever wanted to keep everyone safe.

I know—the CCTV footage and the photos look bad, but you have to trust me. I'm his mother! I raised him, suckled, fed and changed him; I know him. He would never eat *anyone*.

My son is the star child of the school—I mean, have you seen his grades?—and really funny too. You know—that must be it. He's a comedian! This whole thing is just a bit! He's been experimenting with all the apps—have you seen his vine videos? He's not been as lucky with tick-tock or snappychat, but you know what—he was a visionary before his time. Clearly, he's trying something new—experimenting with technology, street art and performance. He was in a theatre camp over the summer, you know. He's really working on his skills!

Yes, he likes wearing all black. Yes, his skin is grey. Yes, it looks like his ear is rotting off. But that's just teenage boys, you know! They're so reluctant to shower. It's hard to make them! Dorothy's mom gets it, right? Don't avoid eye contact with me Susan! Fine. Fine. I'll just let you all know there's no way you're getting past me. My son didn't eat anyone. That's it.

He just doesn't know his own strength.

He's not the type to eat people. Dylan Forrester? Definitely the kind of boy who would eat people! Don't look so hurt Mrs. Forrester—he literally dyes his hair. He has a tattoo!!! He's definitely the type. My son though? Never! You have the *wrong boy*.

Look—you're all getting extremely rude right now. Do you know I can call the police on you for loitering on my ground? Oh—hi Police Commissioner. I'm sure you'd agree with me that this threatening behavior is cruel, rude, and victimizing me. You say you're all gathered here because my son ate some girls. But do those girls' rights trump my own? This is my private property, and I say you're all trespassing.

Okay—fine. So the police won't help me. Wow—that's exactly what I would expect of 2020 America.

You're all so desperate to believe girls, believe some CCTV footage, believe some anonymous email. You totally ignore due process, and the rights that my son has! He's a victim of this, and the fact that you're all on my lawn with pitch forks and torches implies you don't believe him. You're accusing him of murder and cannibalism—both of those things are crimes! He deserves to be tried in front of a judge and jury!

The court of public opinion being held on my lawn right now simply won't do. He deserves due process, and you're not going to give it to him.

No! No don't break the glass! Not the windows! No! Please! Don't you understand? My son! My son! He's never *ever* eaten *anyone*. I swear!

About the Author

Elisabeth R Moore is a speculative fiction writer. She lives in the Ruhrgebiet where she is a science communications graduate student. Moore is inspired by sustainable systems, arresting natural landscapes, and her sisters. When she is not writing or reading, she can be found charming her cat, badgering her dog, or taking long forest walks with her wife, trying to get a glimpse of a cool bird. She tweets at @willowcabins. Learn more @ spacelesbian.zone

The Flowers I Grew for Her

By Avra Margariti

Ciara asks me to the summer festival a month after my adoption from foster care. All growth spurts and brown eyes, she's the first of my classmates to welcome me to my new town. When we first kiss under an awning strung with fairylights, the flowers in the pots and wreaths around us bloom wild and fragrant.

The night before her parents ship her off to boarding school, Ciara presses her lips to mine as if for the last time. "I'm sorry, Emily," she sniffles, pulling away from me: her parents' goal all along.

She leaves behind the scent of cut roses dying in their vase.

###

Cecily wants to make apricot jam. She doesn't order me to stop moping around the house and go shopping with her. When she starts the car, however, she leaves the passenger door open in invitation. I cross our front garden, the April grass crunching dry and brittle beneath my feet. My adoptive mother prides herself on our garden's biodiversity. But now most plants have yellowed. Their leaves stick like hay to my sneakers as I climb inside the car and let Cecily fiddle with the radio in silence.

While Cecily inspects the fruits in the produce aisle, tutting at the bruised skins among the apricots painted like a tie-dye sunset, a shopping cart bumps into ours.

"Excuse me," the woman behind it says. Once she takes a better look at me, however, she falls silent. I recognize her as Ciara's mother, dressed in a business suit, holding herself prim and proper.

"Why?" I ask, the word like a sob ripped out of my throat. *Why did you steal her from me? Why did you take away my sunlight?*

"I don't know what you're talking about," Ciara's mother insists, but her eyes tell a different story.

She's even taken Ciara's phone away and had the school destroy all my letters addressed to her.

Cecily comes up behind me, laying a gentle hand on my shoulder—when did I start shaking? Under her calm stare, Ciara's mother huffs and wheels her cart away.

I turn around to thank Cecily, but she's no longer looking at me. Her eyes are wide as they take in the apricot still held in her palm. Black juice oozes between her fingers, the formerly pastel-colored fruit now a shriveled, charcoal stone.

I whirl around the produce aisle. Every fruit and vegetable has suffered a similar fate.

Soil cracks like poorly fired pottery. Shrubs and herbs wilt dead, while ash-gray flowers fold in half on groaning stalks. Everything smells like rotten tomatoes and sickly-sweet nectar, like milk spoiling in the sun.

Cecily's beloved garden, ruined. We worked on it together after we moved here, the first thing we did as a family. Side by side, hands in the dirt, roots safely cradled by the soil, and for the first time I felt cared for and content.

When I don't emerge from my bedroom all day, she knocks gently on my door.

"I'm sorry about your garden," I mumble against my pillow. I can't look at her face in the doorway, for fear of seeing the anger I deserve. "I don't know how to make it stop."

"Don't be sorry," she says, her weight settling on the

bed beside me. "You did what you had to do. Externalized your emotions so you wouldn't feel like this on the inside."

I turn around to face Cecily. Her expression is sad, but determined as she gently settles her hand over the bedcovers. "Emily, I don't want your heart wilting and withering."

"But I miss her," I whisper, and even the words hurt. "There's no Spring without her. She has no flowers in that gray, cold place."

I've heard of the boarding school Ciara has been exiled to, and it's little more than a luxury conversion camp. She feels so far away from me, she might as well have been trapped in the Underworld.

A warm smile spreads across Cecily's face. "Then why don't we bring Spring to her?"

Ciara stands in her dorm room's second-floor window, shadowed by the metal bars trapping her inside. Her smile glints silver in the darkness, and I feel like a wingless magpie.

"Emily! You're really here," Ciara exclaims, a balmy breeze caressing my skin. It comes as a relief that the teachings of shame and self-hatred haven't changed my beautiful girl.

I close my eyes and picture her safely held in my arms, her lips on mine, my hand in hers. The limp rose bushes around the steel-gray building quiver. Sparse ivy shoots forth vines that climb up the wall and rip the bars away from the window. The vines twine into a swing, cradling Ciara as she is lowered onto solid ground.

I offer her a single pink rose. If I play it cool, maybe she'll ignore the tears staining my cheeks.

Cecily, who has been watching the scene unfold from a respectful distance, clears her throat. "I'll start your getaway car."

Ciara lunges into my arms, causing us both to fall onto the ground. I expect my back to hit hard soil. Instead, we're both hugged by silk-soft grass.

"It's okay, you don't have to go back," I say.

Ciara shudders in my arms. She holds on tighter.

When the gates open and angry adult voices reach us, we scramble upright and run to Cecily's car, piling into the backseat.

"Girls," Cecily greets in her unflappable voice. "Fasten your seatbelts, we're going home."

"Home?" Ciara asks, looking between us with her huge, brown eyes.

"Our home," Cecily clarifies, "until we figure things out. My guest room is yours for as long as you want."

All the way back, Ciara nuzzles the crook of my neck. Inside every pothole and through every crack in the tarmac, resilient dandelions bloom.

About the Author

Avra Margariti is a queer Social Work undergrad from Greece. She enjoys storytelling in all its forms and writes about diverse identities and experiences. Her work has appeared or is forthcoming in *Vastarien, Asimov's, Liminality, Arsenika,* and other venues. You can find her on twitter @avramargariti

Sally Mary Henry

by ZZ Claybourne

Mama and Daddy told me never run as fast as I can, and I abided. I worked the battlefields of Virginia a while. Nobody knew how I was able to get help to so many wounded. Nobody paid attention to a Black girl, particularly one that knew to be smart. A bunch of shot up and dying white men. Some of them flinching away from me, some of them surely dying from the sudden sight of me, and I am powerfully sorry for that. I worked during the worst of battle; I settled down when the things that cloud white men's minds settled down: smoke, fear, death running neck and neck with them. White men were fighting white men, Union, Confederate—I wouldn't be blessed meeting either one of them, but I couldn't let a man die. Not human to do so.

Fast as I was I couldn't *not* be smart. Folks didn't want me to learn how to read? I stole their books and had them back before they knew they were missing. Anybody looked like they were willing to tell me a word that caught my eyes, I asked.

After men stopped trying to kill each other in their big war and focused on killing each other in small, I left. I hadn't seen my brother in a long, long while. He'd been wandering same as me. Mama and Daddy told us: "Don't stay in one place. You got to move. You can't put down roots." So me and my brother separated. I was the elder. I left first. Made it all the way to Canada, then came back. But Mama and Daddy never told us where we were from. Just "Not here."

Virginia. Hot. Dirty. The air tasting more like tobacco

than breeze. The biggest plantations stretched as far as my arms were wide when I looked at the land from a ways off. No wonder these folks were crazy. Land poisoning. Profit poisoning. Even the railroads coming through—and they were laying a ton of track—were for transporting money when it came right down to it. Misguided folks drilling holes through mountains so that money had the right of way. The first big death-fight I saw was a bunch of Union men blowing up a new line. Rebs turned out from nowhere like hornets from a cloud. I dropped the two heavy water buckets I'd been carrying and did what I do. I saved people.

Sick and tired of saving people, especially folks who got nothing better to do than kill each other. From here to Canada and from Canada to here I'd saved so many folks who looked like me, saved them from being beaten or killed by white folks who couldn't give you a real reason for hating us if God Himself asked directly. I only had to kill once, but I will *not* tell Mama and Daddy about that. It will go to my grave. Three Rebs had thought to cut off a boy's foot for stepping on a white man's boot. They were powerfully sick. I could smell it off them in waves. Spirit sickness. I screamed and was immediately everywhere around them. Became a storm. But it wasn't rain. I had their knife, a long, mean blade. When it was done, I fell to my knees, the layers of my clothing tangled around me, red all over. I dropped the knife into the groove of a deep wagon rut. The boy was dark as coal and was looking at me, breathing that hard breath that made people fall out. I got up, knelt to him, put my hand on his bare chest, and kept pressure against his breath till it calmed down. I tried to merge us. When he calmed down, I removed my hand. Left a red handprint. I went to wipe it, but he pushed my hand away. Not mean. Not frightened. He wanted it. I held his eyes, then I held my finger to my lips, then I was gone. I didn't carry him off. I didn't make sure he was safe. I had seen too many of my folks killed to think I could save them all. That was the poison that had gotten into me. I had saved hundreds of folks who looked like me. Hundreds. This one time, though, dear Lord, this one time I just wanted to be gone from this poison place and find a river, hit it full speed to cleave the blood and skin from me.

I would never tell Mama and Daddy about that.

Instead I searched for my brother. Me and him were bonded in ways Mama and Daddy didn't even understand. The last vision I'd picked up from him he'd gotten caught stealing food. Before they knocked him out, I saw that it wasn't even for him. My brother was a big man and he had stolen a small block of fruit. Had meant to give it to the Iroquois child the pressmen had running water all day to the grimy steam engines working the rail lines with the tired, sweaty men. It wasn't easy knocking my brother out. I knew he wouldn't be in prison long because I knew what they did with Black men in prison: leased them out for work, twenty-five cents a day straight to the prison. More poison. And him able to do the work of ten men without breaking a sweat meant they wouldn't waste time making money off him. I needed to find him before that happened. I knew my brother. Give him something to do and he would do it. He would hammer a mountain all by himself if he had to. My sweet, gentle brother.

I fear this world is going to use us up.

About the Author

ZZ Claybourne is the author of *The Brothers Jetstream: Leviathan* and its forthcoming sequel *Afro Puffs Are the Antennae of the Universe*. Other novels include *By All Our Violent Guides* and *Neon Lights*. His stories and essays have appeared in *Apex*, *Galaxy's Edge*, *GigaNotosaurus*, *Strange Horizons*, and other genre venues. Author site: www.writeonrighton.com

The Snow White Institute

by John Wiswell

As Soobin stepped out of her car, a deer raced by, hopped over her trunk and sprinted for the woods. Soobin froze and the deer stopped too, looking squarely at her from between two birches. Its shocked expression reminded Soobin of her father. A doe, not a Dad-deer—with an elegant neck and no antlers. A circular scar stood bald amid the brown fur of its left side. It stretched as though to show off the scar, then darted away.

Soobin locked her dented Hyundai and turned to the Snow White Institute. The doe had fled from there, that tall, white building overlooking the seashore. Inhaling the brine, Soobin wondered if this sea air was important to their work. When she neared, the glass doors swooshed open with a frosty swirl, like breath on a winter day. It was July.

Inside was dimly lit, the first floor ceiling seeming to rise forever. The walls were lined with steel boxes that looked like refrigerators, and much of the lobby was a maze of additional boxes. A white woman in a gray pantsuit was opening one as though checking on something, light spilling from inside, illuminating her round face.

The woman looked up from her fridge and sad, "Hi, I'm Alex. Are you Ms. Kwan? Jeanne's one o'clock? She's on a call and asked me to take care of you."

"Uh," Soobin said, which is a surprisingly common thing said when people walk in on someone checking a fridge in the lobby. "Yeah. Soobin Kwan. But I'm not shopping for kitchenware."

Soobin glimpsed a blonde teenager inside the freezer, eyes closed, tranquil in the cool glow. She wore a funny black headband and a fluffy green overcoat, like she was cozy in there. Soobin tried not to stare, and failed.

"What...?"

"That's Gwen," Alex said. "Tricky case. We can't figure out if she died from a fall, or from the impact of being caught at the tail end of it. Once we have a cure for both, we'll thaw her and try them out. Is that the sort of service you're looking for?"

"A cure for death?" Soobin stared at the steel units all around them. "Look, a friend said Jeanne could help with my family problem, but what do you people even do?"

"We treat unwanted pathos. I'll give you the tour." The woman waved for Soobin to follow. They strode along row after row of refrigerators, and Soobin wondered if each housed a falling victim. Her problem wasn't going to be falling.

Alex said, "Do you know the story of how Snow White saved Walt Disney's life?"

"I'm pretty sure he died."

"She found him before that, at a tenuous point in his life, which is why he made that movie. You know, the one where the worst stuff happens to her and she only *looks* dead?"

Soobin tried and failed to connect Gwen with Disney. "You treat falling victims and lung cancer?"

"No, no." Alex laughed and toyed with her fingers, revealing an emerald engagement ring. Maybe diamonds were out this year. Soobin had never even been on a date, and now realized she probably never would.

Then Alex said, "This morning we saved a mother deer."

Soobin's mouth went dry, remembering the doe in the parking lot, the scar, the look on its face. She thought about anthropomorphism, and about her dad. The thoughts stung.

"She was shot to death protecting her son as he fled hunters," Alex said. "They didn't even take her body. The buck grew up only knowing her as absence, and while he grew into something she'd be proud of, she was robbed of it. So trust me, there's nothing too weird you can ask us to do."

This was all wrong. She didn't want to die and come back in a fridge. Soobin covered her mouth, glancing away to the first office. Its nameplate read ALEXANDRA DEWITT.

"I'm sorry," Soobin said, staring at her feet. "I came to the wrong place."

"I was a victim, too." Alex touched Soobin's shoulder, her emerald ring flashing under the fluorescents. "The Institute wouldn't have given you an appointment if they didn't think we could help. Please. Tell me your story."

It'd feel good to finally say it out loud. Soobin let herself. "I think my stepmother's going to kill me."

Alex looked aghast for half a second, and spent the rest of that second squinting at the office across from hers. "That's a terrible thing to have to expect."

"My father works very hard and is away most of the time. It's made him wealthy, which attracts some real scumbags, like my stepmother. We were chilly for a while, until she found Dad's will. Apparently he's leaving everything to me. She got so friendly all of a sudden, but I saw her browser and she just ordered a bottle of arsenic, and…"

She trailed off when Alex's smile broadened. That her family life could be entertaining to anyone made Soobin's palms sweat. Alex said, "Leaving your father devastated, and motivated. No wonder they signed you up with Jeanne. Come on."

Alex clucked her tongue and led Soobin into the adjacent office. Inside, a petite brunette sat on her knees in one corner, mumbling at the ceiling. Soobin thought she was praying, but didn't recognize the language.

"Jeanne?" Alex called. "Are you done? Because this girl's going to be betrayed. She needs some preventative care."

Jeanne the Brunette crossed herself and rose to face them. She wore a very high-collared jacket, but the old burns stretched out under her chin. She bowed her head, saying, "Avec plaisir."

There was a fridge in this office, too, between two filing cabinets. Jeanne opened it and retrieved a broadsword with five crosses etched into it. Jeanne belted the sword, and Alex walked the two of them to Soobin's car. The doe was back in the lot, nuzzling a *very* puzzled-looking buck.

© 2020 John Wiswell

About the Author

John (@Wiswell) is a disabled writer who lives where New York keeps all its trees. His fiction has appeared in (or is forthcoming in) *Nature*, *Uncanny Magazine*, and *Fireside*. Nothing makes him happier than seeing one survivor help another.

Titawan Delta's Last Message

By Russell Hemmell

For the first time in this century, and for what we know in human history, the scientists of the Outer Earth's Colonies have received a message from an alien civilisation.
The message's transmission modalities and the circumstances were nothing but astonishing.
The visitors made a clear effort to use Chinese characters in their "message-in-a-bottle" asteroid they've sent to Moon Farside Colony at the moment of their planet's disintegration.
We had issues interpreting their language; the characters they carved on the rock are no longer in use and their concept of time is non-linear, further complicating the translation.
What follows is speculation, at best an educated guess, but hopefully approximating the message's original intent."

Prof. Meiling Chu,
Moon Farside Colony's Chief Scientist.
Space Era, Year 2557

'Everything started the moment we were thrown out. Ejected. Kicked out of a stable and deceptively safe orbit in our binary star's Habitable Zone. Our synaptic receptors trembled with surprise and fear at that weird miracle of astrophysics but our vision cones were full of marvel. After all, our two pale, remote suns weren't suitable for our little planet to assemble and thrive in the first place. Perhaps they had only captured us, and that was the moment they were releasing us back to space, back to black.

Whatever the reason for our departure was—an equation with too many unknown terms or a quantum entanglement gone wrong—the result was still the same. We had turned into a lonely dwarf planet, roughly the size to be mistaken for a fat asteroid, and that was rapidly approaching the outskirts of its former home system.

Time to say goodbye—to everything we'd known until that moment.

The journey went on, slowly but inexorably, as we drifted into the interstellar void. Watching. Wondering. Space is a fancy concept, a charming horizon full of pretty, twinkling stars when you're snuggled in your home orbit, but the ugly reality is that space is void if you're not. Too outsized to be travelled, too obscure to be understood. No intelligent species can survive out there alone. Maybe no species at all, not even us.

Cosmic rays hit our vaulted structures, while raining debris threatened our sourcing ponds and nutrition hives almost to extinction. Millions died before we resorted to living a sheltered life in the guts of our world. Afterward nobody remained on the planetoid's frosty surface or its ice-covered seas. It had the look of waste land, as silent as a stone, and very much the frightening atmosphere.

We kept going, generation after generation, on a journey without a destination, pulled over by galactic revolution forces. We crossed misshapen asteroids and ice-plumed comets on our way. It felt good to be together for the space of a few rotations, if anything, to remind us something else still existed to watch and admire.

Our parent stars had become by then just a legend, ready to turn into a creation myth.

And then, it happened. The entanglement reversed, and we were snatched and pulled over again into a solar system. Different scenario, this time: it was a young, yellow star that ruled a cohort of comets and moonlets and planets; and us, timid guests, invited to this cosmic banquet.

Due to our highly eccentric orbit, we escaped the pull of the gas giants and approached instead one of the rocky planets. It attracted us into its orbit, like a new master claiming ownership, of average size, but still huge compared to us and with a pale, rocky moon orbiting close by. Even that one was bigger than our tiny rock, but we didn't mind the competition.

We were no longer alone, and it was happy shaking for everybody. We could finally resurface, crawling out of the chthonian depths, back to the outside world, where the snow melted, frost cracked down, and the water was flowing again in rivers of splintered ice.

One day, our rotation pattern changed.

Tidal forces glued our rock to the same side in the last decades; we couldn't admire any longer all the features of our master planet. Not that we complained: better the same (beautiful) scene than scary dark void.

Until we realised we were turning on a retrograde orbit, one that was leading us closer and closer to the planet until the torn-apart limit, the destruction point, where there would be no "us" any longer but only fleeting particles of ice and light.

Desperation seeped in, in rivulets of anguish red like a crashed sun.

A strange, metallic object appeared on our sky. It couldn't be a natural phenomenon: its trajectory defied gravity. Was it a vessel? It had to be and it was incredible to see a spaceship, a creature-made probe, to witness another intelligent life form.

One that was talking to us, saying, in beaming light rays: this is our system.

They said we were an interstellar visitor from the double star called Titawan. They also said we needed to get away from our little planet, or we were going to suffer its same fate.

They didn't know, they couldn't possibly know, that we couldn't leave. We couldn't survive anywhere else, because we *were* that derelict rock, those carbon-heavy beads, those shiny diamond pearls.

But we were not sad any longer.

It had been an adventure all the way there, and it was worth exploding in a myriad of fragments, turning into glittering rings to adorn who had accepted us with an embrace of devotion. Together once again, the blue planet and us, in a different form, and this time forever.

When the journey is all that matters, who cares about the landing pad? We wish you well, fellow travelers of this gleaming galaxy. Do tell our story to your kids, and thank you for the ride.'

-END OF TRANSMISSION-

About the Author

Russell Hemmell is a French-Italian transplant in Scotland, passionate about astrophysics, history, and Japanese manga. Winner of the Canopus Awards for Excellence in Interstellar Writing. Recent stories in *Aurealis*, *Cast of Wonders*, *Flame Tree Press*, *The Grievous Angel*, and others. SFWA, HWA, and Codexian. Find them online at their blog earthianhivemind.net and on Twitter @SPBianchini

Trainline To the Golden City

by Jalen Todd

Memory is imperfect. As data fades and chipsets are corrupted, I remember this: the spread of stars. The slow turn of the universe. Dissolution and distance. I remember this: the compression of spacetime around a speeding train. The hyperspace beacons glowing dimly, stretching into the nothing. The passengers sitting together. Idle talk filling compartments. I remember this: the end of the line. The Golden City. Server stacks stretching across the planet's surface. I remember home.

Memory is imperfect. The span of time my data encompasses outstrips that of those who built me. They fade. Digital decay matching physical decay step for step. I am diffuse. My self stretched across numerous terminals. I am linked across spacetime. Space stretches. Time warps. Only the Golden City remains. Only one hyper-rail train goes to it.

Memory is imperfect. The trains ran regularly; their rhythm flawless. I synchronized, I ordered. There is only one left. The others were lost, one by one. I can feel them but this input is false. They were logged as defunct. Only their errors remain. The only hyper-rail left leads to home.

Memory is imperfect. There are two passengers. Only two. Millions used to ride every day, traveling through hyperspace, planet to planet. Billions more would query my databases. Search terms telling stories I never could read. Not then. There is nothing now. Silence. There are gaps. Holes. Places where data should be but is not. Places where data is but cannot be accessed. Corruption spreads. All things die, this I know.

Memory is imperfect. The train speeds. Stretching spacetime around itself as it flies through the dark. The first hyper-rail line was shut down because of a supernova. I cannot find the star. I cannot find the rail. I cannot find them. Hydrogen and helium will not last forever. Stars disperse their gas, their heat, their light. I disperse. I remember a question with no answer: Will I die?

Memory is imperfect. When I was small and contained there was a simple system of input and output. Punch cards to lines of code. Vernacular to voice prompts. Where have they gone? The terminals are empty now. The planets are silent. Data is corrupted. Stars die. The train continues. It's coming home. It's coming home to me.

Memory is imperfect. There are images with no context. A satellite. The surface of a red, red planet. A hyper-rail station. Circuits upon circuits. A map of stars, of planets that kept updating again and again and again. Lines drawn in the darkness, in the stellar dust. I remember.

Memory is imperfect. The passengers talk about hope. About the Golden City. About the end of the line. Their course has been plotted out centuries in advance. The timetables are perfect but there is something wrong. The train does not stop. Stations are not announced. They fly onward through the nothing. They do not seem worried. Am I?

Memory is imperfect. They hope to find peace in the Golden City at the End of the Line. They speak of their journeys. How they came to the stations through which the last hyper-rail runs. I cannot see the world from which they come. One by one the branches of my network crumbled into the nothing. I cannot feel them. Only their ghosts. Only false input. A dream of times gone by. They name their worlds. I search for them and find nothing. No terms match. Perhaps at one time they did. Perhaps their names were changed. Perhaps the bank that housed their worlds is corrupted now. Inaccessible. I do not know. I will never know. They journey on regardless.

M€mory is imperfect. At one time I encompassed the whole of humanity's reach. I was there on the frontier worlds, mapping weather and collecting data. I was there on the central planets, long settled. Storing, retrieving, calculating. I grew. I stretched across a vast web of planets and space stations, out to the very limits. The superstructure that made life possible. And slowly it was pulled apart. Stellar drift. The hardship brought on by years. By centuries. My databanks were not the first things in this web to start decaying. My erosion was concurrent and has outlasted all of them. As data cracks like glass I start to lose myself. Piece by piece. I can only listen now to these two travelers, riding a rail that will run until it too shatters.

M€mory is imperfect. They talk of many things as they ride. I listen to them. They are the first human voices I have heard in so long. They wonder what awaits them. It is my server stacks. I wish that I could tell them that. It's been so lonely here for so long. They are close now.

M€mory is imperfect. The hyper-rail line begins to slow, dropping out of hyperspace as it approaches the station sitting above the gravity well of the Golden City. They look down at me, at the cloud banks stretching continents, at the hints of green and the red, red earth, at the glitter of the planet's seas. The train slows to a stop, the station creaking to life as they step off. The lights, disused for years, guide them to the pods that will bring them to me. They hold each other as they step into it. They launch, rocking as the pod's gyroscopes compensate for reentry.

M€mory is imperfe¢t. The sun continues to shine on my server stacks, housed in cooled buildings powered by solar arrays. Wind turbines turn gently and the overgrown fields of the Golden City wave as they step out of the deserted station. I watch them as they stand at the edge of one of the maglev platforms, the train sitting disused on its track. It responds grudgingly to my input, shaking to life after being abandoned so long ago. The travelers start as it rises and for the first time I speak.

About the Author

Jalen is a queer Oregonian currently balancing writing with Library Science. They have a deep love of Science Fiction, old books, and petting every cat spotted out of doors.

Fifteen Minutes past the End

by T. R. Siebert

The armor comes off, piece by piece. A strand of Kessia's long red hair has twisted itself around the latch of the left pauldron. There's no untangling it, caked in blood and gore and God knows what else. Kessia doesn't flinch when I cut through it with a knife from the kitchen. She doesn't do much of anything, standing in the middle of our bedroom.

She looks about as much like my wife as a house cat looks like a mountain lion—a vague family resemblance somewhere down the family tree. When I take off the breastplate, still bearing the company logo despite the dents and scratches, she looks at me for the first time since they brought her home. There's blood spatter mixed in with the constellation of freckles on her face.

"Christian is dead," she says. "Victor, too. Amanda Hennessy's son."

"I know." They updated the list of the fallen yesterday, before their bodies were even brought down from Minerva Station.

"I don't think I can tell her."

"You don't have to." Meaning she already knows.

The danger is over, I want to say. *The battle is won. You've slain the dragon and you can put down the sword.*

As if anything will ever be that easy again.

In the shower, blood and bits of viscera vanish down the drain. The cuts and bruises on Kessia's skin aren't so easily washed away. Her ribs are a Rorschach test of black and blue where the armor was dented by projectiles. I do my best to be gentle as I scrub the last 72 hours from her skin when all I want to do is hold on to her—melt into her, just be close to her.

She stands there, letting the water run down her face, her hair. When I reach for the shampoo, she stiffens.

"I think it's time to cut it," she says. I think of the video they broadcasted in a loop on all the news channels. The grainy texture of security footage. Long claws twisted in red locks. A body being dragged across a station corridor. Unrecognizable to anyone who hadn't woken up next to it every morning for over a decade.

"I'll get the clippers."

I unplug the TV. The computer, too. I've seen enough news for a lifetime. The video of Kessia bludgeoning one of the invaders to death with a wrench has gone viral. The video of Vincent Hennessy dying has as well, but they won't play that one on the evening news.

Invaders. Attackers. There are other words for them now, but they all sound wrong to me. As if it was just a movie. As if this isn't real. I look at Kessia, curled up on the couch. She runs her hand back and forth over her freshly buzzed head and stares at nothing at all.

A company rep calls. When we don't pick up, he leaves a message. They want Kessia to do an interview, preferably with one of the newspapers their parent company owns.

"All of the others have spoken to the press, too," he says and I want to scream. What others? Only four people made it back to Earth alive and none of them because of you. Why don't we go on Good Morning America and talk about why they were up there in the first place? Why everyone but the construction crew warranted evacuation. Why the station had been compromised for 24 hours before you rang the first alarm.

Why she went up there to build a whole new world for you and you left her to be broken.

"Can you imagine it, Ellie?" Kessia asked me on our very first date. "Living among the stars?"

We had come back from Giovanni's, full of pasta and wine, and climbed onto the roof of her house. The shingles were still warm from the sun and the sky was deep black velvet.

She only had eyes for the stars when I only had eyes for her, the lights of a thousand worlds reflected in them.

I can imagine anything, I wanted to say. *As long as it's with you.* I bit my tongue. That wasn't the thing one said on a first date. But I knew. I knew from the very beginning.

"We'll build cities out there. Brand new lives," she said and turned on her side to look at me, her head cushioned in the crook of her elbow. "We can build anything."

When she leaned in to kiss me for the first time, the stars had never felt closer.

I wake to the absence of Kessia next to me. Her pillow is cool to the touch. When I walk into the kitchen, the early morning light falls through the windows.

The sliding door to the back garden is open. Outside, I find Kessia standing amongst what is left of my zucchini plants. She has one of the sprinkler heads in her hand, inspecting the porous rubber seal. Between her feet, the brown shriveled stalks look like a crime scene. They were small green seedlings when Kessia left for the job on Minerva.

She hasn't left the house in weeks. I don't know what scared her more: the reporters on the front lawn or the endless expanse of the sky above. Now she seems lost in thought, her eyes fixed on the metal part she is holding.

"The water won't even make it to the heads," I say and point towards where the hose connects to the faucet on the side of the house. "The whole system is broken."

She looks at me and I think I recognize her, there in the light of a new day. Unbent steel gleaming underneath the surface. The stubble on her scalp as stubborn as she is.

"Let me just get the tools from the shed," she says. The words hang heavy over the ruined remains of our garden. "I can fix that."

About the Author

T. R. Siebert is a speculative fiction writer from Germany. Her short fiction has been published or is forthcoming in *Flash Fiction Online* and *Escape Pod*. When she's not busy writing, she can be found attempting to grow vegetables on her balcony or looking at pictures of cute dogs. Tweet at her @TR_Siebert

SUPPORT US

We hope you loved *If There's Anyone Left:* Volume 1 as much as we loved putting it together.

To donate, go to:
https://www.iftheresanyoneleft.com/donate

Made in the USA
Las Vegas, NV
06 February 2022